The Summer Nick Taught His Cats to Read

Curtis Manley   *Illustrated by* Kate Berube

A Paula Wiseman Book
Simon & Schuster Books for Young Readers
New York   London   Toronto   Sydney   New Delhi

For Frances, and for my parents
—C. M.

For my sister, Camie, who taught *me* how to read
—K. B.

SIMON & SCHUSTER BOOKS FOR YOUNG READERS
An imprint of Simon & Schuster Children's Publishing Division • 1230 Avenue of the Americas, New York, New York 10020
Text copyright © 2016 by Curtis Manley • Illustrations copyright © 2016 by Kate Berube • All rights reserved, including
the right of reproduction in whole or in part in any form. • SIMON & SCHUSTER BOOKS FOR YOUNG READERS is a
trademark of Simon & Schuster, Inc. • For information about special discounts for bulk purchases, please contact Simon &
Schuster Special Sales at 1-866-506-1949 or business@simonandschuster.com. • The Simon & Schuster Speakers Bureau can
bring authors to your live event. For more information or to book an event, contact the Simon & Schuster Speakers Bureau at
1-866-248-3049 or visit our website at www.simonspeakers.com. • Book design by Chloë Foglia • The text for this book was
set in New Century Schoolbook. • The illustrations for this book were rendered in ink, Flashe paint, and acrylic paint on cold
press watercolor paper. • Manufactured in China • 0416 SCP • First Edition
10 9 8 7 6 5 4 3 2 1
Library of Congress Cataloging-in-Publication Data
Manley, Curtis, author.
The summer Nick taught his cats to read / Curtis Manley ; illustrated by Kate Berube.—1st edition.
pages cm
"A Paula Wiseman Book."
Summary: When Nick decides to teach his cats to read, Verne is very much
interested, especially in books about mice and fish, but Stevenson wants
nothing to do with the project—or does he?
ISBN 978-1-4814-3569-7 (hardcover)—ISBN 978-1-4814-3570-3 (eBook)
[1.Books and reading—Fiction. 2. Cats—Fiction. 3. Illustration
of books—Fiction.]
I. Berube, Kate, illustrator. II. Title.
PZ7.1.M365Sum 2016
[E]—dc23
2014024861

Nick had two cats, Verne and Stevenson.

They spent summers doing everything together.

But when Nick sat down with a book, the cats had their own ideas.

So Nick decided to teach them to read. He started with easy words.

"Ball!" said Nick. "B-A-L-L."
But the cats just wanted to play.

At lunchtime Nick pointed
at the word *food*.

FOOD

BEE
F
MAT
CUP
Bug
AF
ANT

The cats ignored him.

"Wake up!" said Nick after they fell asleep.
"This is no time for an N-A-P!"

His cats did not like that at all.

So Nick made new flash cards—
and Verne got interested.

But not Stevenson.

Stevenson just said "Mrrp," and crawled under the bed.

Nick tried nursery rhymes next. When he read "Three Little Kittens," Verne searched everywhere for mittens.

But not Stevenson.

Then Nick read his favorite books to Verne, who liked stories about cats and stories about fish. Verne *loved* fish. He followed along as Nick read, learning the sounds of the letters.

Verne practiced on his own, over and over, even after Nick went to bed. Soon he was reading new stories all by himself.

The next morning, Nick tried once more. "F-I-S-H. See? *Fish!* Verne loves that word. Don't you?" But Stevenson said, "Meow!" and ran under the porch. He hissed at Nick and Verne.

Verne got his own library card
and borrowed so many books
that Nick could hardly carry
them home.

When they discovered a story they both liked, they acted out their favorite scenes.

They dug up fish fossils in the flower bed.

They bounced across the surface of the Moon.

It was fun, but it would have been more fun with Stevenson.

Then Verne discovered a treasure under the bed— a great stack of Stevenson's pirate drawings. "Wow!" Nick whispered. "Stevenson drew a story."

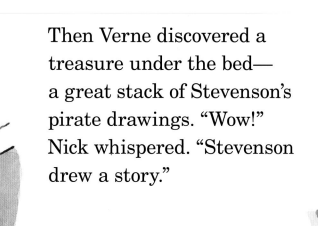

"We should write the words,"
said Nick. Verne helped.

When they were done, they squeezed under the porch,
gave Stevenson an eye patch, and read *The Tale of
One-Eyed Stevenson and the Pirate Gold.*

Stevenson listened and followed along. He didn't run
away. Or hiss. Not even once.

So Nick and Verne took him to the
library to find more books.

The next morning when Nick woke up, Stevenson
already had his whiskers in a book.

When Verne and Nick needed help fighting pirates,
Stevenson found a sword too.
"Welcome aboard, matey!" Nick yelled. "Step lively!"

Nick and Verne rounded up two scurvy mutineers.

And Stevenson held them at bay.

Then Nick and Verne climbed the mast and looked out over Treasure Island. When Nick yelled, "Land ho!" Stevenson was right there with them.

Then they all hurried down and waded ashore—and it was
Stevenson who found the buried treasure.

Now Nick and his cats hunt for dinosaurs
in the lost world behind the garden.

They race around the yard in eighty seconds.

They journey to the center of the basement.

Sometimes Verne and Stevenson curl up with their own books, and sometimes Nick reads to them while they close their eyes and purr.

But Nick also likes it when
someone reads to him.

"Maybe I should teach you how to speak," he
says to his cats. "How hard could that be?"

"Meow!" says Stevenson.